WILD WHEELS
MASERATIS

WITHDRAWN

By Bob Power

Gareth Stevens
Publishing

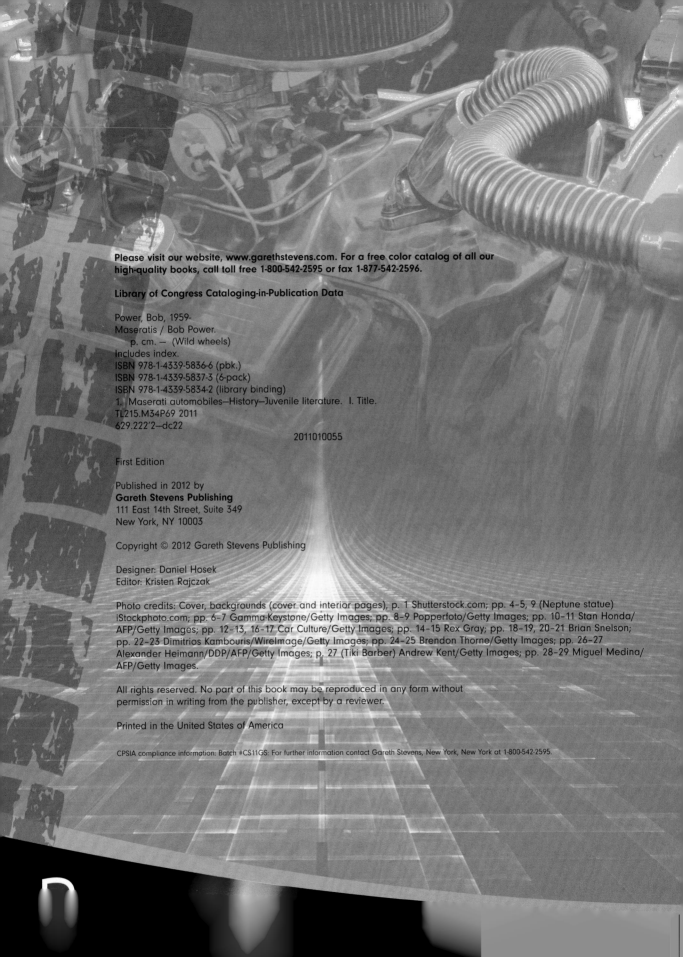

Please visit our website, www.garethstevens.com. For a free color catalog of all our high-quality books, call toll free 1-800-542-2595 or fax 1-877-542-2596.

Library of Congress Cataloging-in-Publication Data

Power, Bob, 1959-
Maseratis / Bob Power.
    p. cm. — (Wild wheels)
Includes index.
ISBN 978-1-4339-5836-6 (pbk.)
ISBN 978-1-4339-5837-3 (6-pack)
ISBN 978-1-4339-5834-2 (library binding)
1. Maserati automobiles—History—Juvenile literature. I. Title.
TL215.M34P69 2011
629.222'2—dc22

2011010055

First Edition

Published in 2012 by
Gareth Stevens Publishing
111 East 14th Street, Suite 349
New York, NY 10003

Designer: Daniel Hosek
Editor: Kristen Rajczak

Photo credits: Cover, backgrounds (cover and interior pages), p. 1 Shutterstock.com; pp. 4–5, 9 (Neptune statue) iStockphoto.com; pp. 6–7 Gamma-Keystone/Getty Images; pp. 8–9 Popperfoto/Getty Images; pp. 10–11 Stan Honda/AFP/Getty Images; pp. 12–13, 16–17 Car Culture/Getty Images; pp. 14–15 Rex Gray; pp. 18–19, 20–21 Brian Snelson; pp. 22–23 Dimitrios Kambouris/WireImage/Getty Images; pp. 24–25 Brendon Thorne/Getty Images; pp. 26–27 Alexander Heimann/DDP/AFP/Getty Images; p. 27 (Tiki Barber) Andrew Kent/Getty Images; pp. 28–29 Miguel Medina/AFP/Getty Images.

Printed in the United States of America

CPSIA compliance information: Batch #CS11GS: For further information contact Gareth Stevens, New York, New York at 1-800-542-2595.

CONTENTS

Words in the glossary appear in **bold** type the first time
they are used in the text.

Always Changing, Always Fast

Have you ever ridden in a really fast car? Fast cars can be fun and exciting. One of the world's fastest cars is the Maserati MC12. This speedy car can zip along at more than 200 miles (322 km) per hour!

The MC12 is one of a long line of Maseratis. The Maserati brothers started the company in Italy during the early 1900s. Since then, Maseratis have competed on many racetracks and become some of the most revered cars in the world. Though the company has gone through many changes over the years, it continues to make fast, exciting cars.

INSIDE THE MACHINE

Only 50 Maserati MC12s were ever produced. They're very fast and powerful. MC12s can go from 0 to 62 miles (100 km) per hour in just 3.8 seconds. They're expensive, too. The original price for a new MC12 was more than $800,000!

Many Maserati models, such as this GranTurismo, are created with the buyer's help. The buyer often chooses the car's color and even the kind of wood used on the door panels!

The Maserati Brothers

The Maserati story began in Voghera, a town in northern Italy. There, Rodolfo Maserati and Carolina Losi Maserati had seven sons. Sadly, one died as a baby. The sons that survived were Carlo, Bindo, Alfieri, Mario, Ettore, and Ernesto. The oldest son, Carlo, was born in 1881. Ernesto, the baby of the family, was born in 1898.

Starting with Carlo in 1903, most of the Maserati brothers ended up working for the car company Isotta Fraschini. The brothers held many jobs at the company. Carlo and Alfieri even worked as test drivers for the cars the company made.

INSIDE THE MACHINE

Carlo worked for a bicycle maker and the carmaker Fiat before going to work for Isotta Fraschini. He was so good at his job that the owners of Isotta Fraschini decided they wanted more Maserati brothers working for them. Sadly, Carlo died when he was just 29 years old.

The Maserati team gets ready to start a race in 1931.

The First Maserati

In 1914, after years at Isotta Fraschini, Alfieri Maserati decided to form his own company in Bologna, Italy. The company made car parts. Alfieri also started racing cars. He even helped **design** race cars for the carmaker Diatto.

In 1926, Alfieri's company produced the first true Maserati. Other cars had used Maserati parts, but this was the first car made entirely by the Maserati company. It was also the first to have the company's logo on it. The car was called the Tipo 26. Alfieri drove the car in its first race, the Targa Florio. The car came in first for its **class**.

Even early Maseratis like this one were known for being fast.

While the other Maserati brothers worked with cars, Mario became an artist. He's thought to have designed the Maserati logo. The logo shows a trident, or weapon that looks like a pitchfork. It's based on the trident carried by a statue of the Roman sea god Neptune that stands in the city of Bologna.

Neptune

The Early Years

The 16-**cylinder** Maserati V4 came out in 1929. This powerful race car set a world speed record for its class and helped create the company's image as a first-rate carmaker.

In 1932, Alfieri Maserati died. His brothers Bindo, Ernesto, and Ettore took over Maserati. They continued racing their cars and trying to make them better. In 1937, the brothers sold the company

Michael Schumacher drives a 1938 Maserati race car around the Indianapolis Motor Speedway in 2002.

to the Orsi family, though they stayed on as chief engineers. The company moved to Modena, Italy. This city was home to other sports car makers, including Ferrari and Lamborghini.

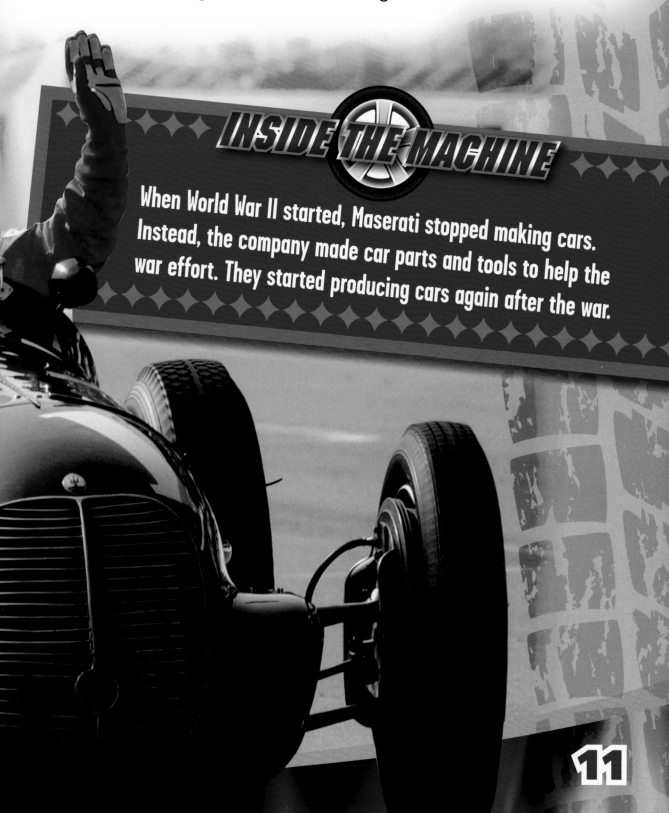

INSIDE THE MACHINE

When World War II started, Maserati stopped making cars. Instead, the company made car parts and tools to help the war effort. They started producing cars again after the war.

Cars for the Road

At first, Maserati made mostly race cars. These were expensive to make but didn't bring in much money. In the 1950s, Maserati started making cars for the road to support the racing division.

Maserati introduced its first widely produced road car in 1957—the 3500 GT. It had a **straight-six** engine designed especially for it.

In 1958, Iran's ruler, the shah, visited Maserati. He liked the 3500 GT but wanted a car that few others would own. So, Maserati created the 5000 GT for him. It was much like the 3500 GT but had a more powerful **V-8** engine. Only 34 were made between 1959 and 1965.

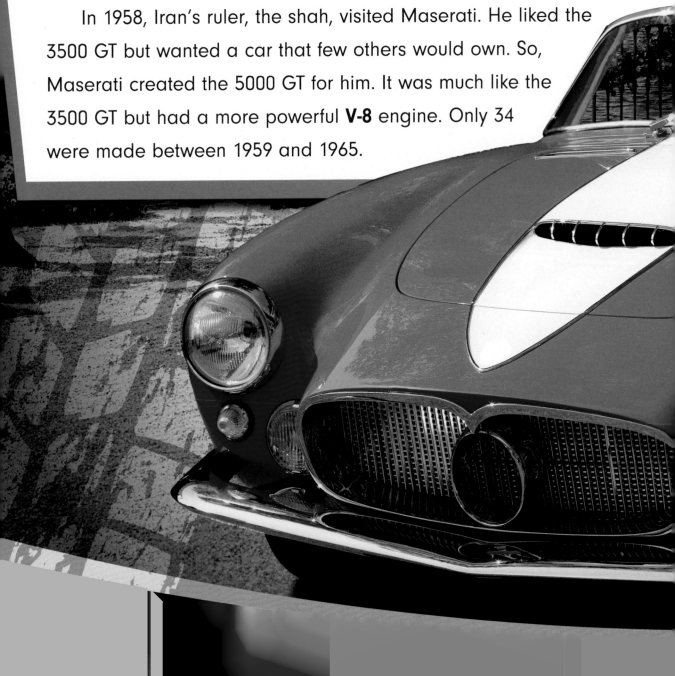

Maserati based another car on the 3500 GT. The Sebring was produced from 1962 to 1969. It was named after Sebring, Florida, where a Maserati had won a major race a few years earlier. The Sebring could go faster than 146 miles (235 km) per hour.

Many of Maserati's first road cars became instant classics! This 1956 Maserati A6 G54 was sleek and stylish.

The Quattroporte and the Mistral

Until 1962, all the cars Maserati made had two doors. That year, the Muslim spiritual leader Prince Karim Aga Khan ordered a car with four doors. The following year, Maserati started selling a four-door car similar to the special one it built for him. They named this new car the Quattroporte, which means "four doors" in Italian. The Quattroporte was a success for Maserati. Over the years, the Quattroporte has been updated several times.

The Mistral was the last Maserati model to use a straight-six engine.

In 1963, the Maserati Mistral was shown at a motor show in Turin, Italy. The original Mistral was a **coupe**, with a hard roof. In 1964, a **convertible** called the Mistral **Spyder** was introduced.

INSIDE THE MACHINE

The Mistral was named after a cold wind that blows from the north or northwest into southern France. All later two-person Maseratis followed the same practice and were named after famous winds.

The Mexico, the Ghibli, and the Indy

Maserati started producing the Mexico in 1966. It had a V-8 engine and a more advanced braking system. Like some earlier Maseratis, the Mexico had two doors and seated four people. It had a luxurious **interior** with leather seats.

In 1967, Maserati started producing a car named after an Egyptian desert wind. The Ghibli coupe boasted a powerful 315-**horsepower** engine and a stylish modern look. The stunning long, low hood and pop-up headlights were the work of a young designer named Giorgetto Giugiaro. In 1969, the Indy replaced the Sebring in the Maserti lineup. It was larger inside and more practical for everyday driving than the sleek Ghibli.

Maserati produced the Ghibli from 1966 to 1973. The name was used again for the Ghibli II from 1992 to 1997.

INSIDE THE MACHINE

The Indy was named after the Indianapolis Motor Speedway, a racetrack near Indianapolis, Indiana. Maserati had twice won the track's famous annual race, the Indianapolis 500. The Indy is one of several four-seat Maseratis named after racetracks.

Maseratis of the 1970s

The Bora, named after a wind along the eastern coast of the Adriatic Sea, was introduced in 1971. It was Maserati's first car with an engine located in the middle of the car. This made the car more powerful. A **hydraulic** system controlled the brakes, driver's seat, and headlights. Giugiaro designed this Maserati as well, and he gave it a stylish look.

Another car with a mid-engine design, the Merak, was introduced at the 1972 auto show in Paris, France. While the Bora had a V-8 engine, the Merak had a smaller V-6 engine. It could reach 149 miles (240 km) per hour.

Two other Maserati models that appeared in the 1970s were the Khamsin and the Kyalami. The Khamsin was named after a hot wind that blows in the deserts of northern Africa. The Kyalami was named after a racetrack in South Africa.

The Merak wasn't named after a wind. Merak is one star in Ursa Major, which is also called the Great Bear or the Big Dipper.

The Biturbo

The Maserati Biturbo appeared in 1981. It had a V-6 engine with two turbochargers. A turbocharger **compresses** air flowing into the cylinders of a car's engine. This allows more air and more fuel to fit into each cylinder, which creates more power as the fuel is burned. Turbochargers are most often found on race cars or really powerful sports cars.

The Biturbo was on *Time* magazine's list of the 50 worst cars of all time.

During the 1980s and early 1990s, several Biturbo models were made. There were spyders, coupes, and four-door cars. While they were less expensive than other Maseratis, many people complained the Biturbos were poorly made.

INSIDE THE MACHINE

The Biturbo didn't sell well in the United States because of the numerous problems owners had with early models. To some car lovers, it ruined Maserati's standing as a carmaker. From 1991 to 2002, the company pulled out of the United States entirely.

A New Century

The Maserati factory in Modena was redesigned in the 1990s. In 1998, Maserati introduced the 3200 GT at the Paris auto show. It was the first car to come out of the redesigned Maserati factory. It had a powerful V-8 engine with twin turbochargers. The car's great new look and beautiful interior came from a familiar source—the company founded by designer Giorgetto Giugiaro. Several cars based on the 3200 GT followed.

The 4200 GT helped fix Maserati's image in the United States.

The Spyder Cambiocorsa came out in 2001. It was Maserati's first road car with a race car–style paddle-shift **gearshift**. This made changing gears easier. The gearshift could be set for quick, racing-style gear changes or even for poor weather conditions.

INSIDE THE MACHINE

The 4200 GT was introduced at the Detroit auto show in 2002. This marked Maserati's return to the United States. The car had a new V-8 engine designed and produced for Maserati by Ferrari.

The GranTurismo

In 2007, Maserati came out with the GranTurismo. This powerful new sports car had a 405-horsepower V-8 engine. It also had a comfortable, roomy interior that seated four people. The car's body was carefully balanced and **aerodynamic**. It was even tested in a wind tunnel!

The GranTurismo's look was based on a **concept car** called the Birdcage 75th that Maserati built in 2005. Several GranTurismo models followed. One was the GranTurismo MC, which was designed for racing.

INSIDE THE MACHINE

Owners of the GranTurismo could add extra features from the MC Sport Line to their cars. Many of these features were made of a light material called carbon fiber. Features from the MC Sport Line could be added to Quattroportes from the 2000s, too.

Many people liked the way the GranTurismo drove. It could produce 405 horsepower!

Famous Drivers

Lots of rich and famous people have owned Maseratis over the years. They include football player Tiki Barber, actor and wrestler Dwayne "the Rock" Johnson, and former US president Ronald Reagan. Musicians of all kinds have owned Maseratis, too. Bono, the singer of the band U2, owned a Quattroporte. The opera singer Luciano Pavarotti owned a Sebring 4.0 and a Quattroporte.

Other people became famous as the drivers of Maserati race cars. Some stars from the company's team include Cesare Perdisa, Sergio Mantovani, and Giorgio Scarlatti. Argentina's Juan Manuel Fangio raced for several companies during the 1950s, including Maserati. Some people think that Fangio was the best race-car driver ever.

This Quattroporte was introduced at the International Motor Show in _____ in 2003.

INSIDE THE MACHINE

Maseratis have been used in lots of movies, such as *Rocky III*, *Rocky V*, *Underworld*, and *Charlie's Angels: Full Throttle*. Characters in lots of different TV shows, from *CSI* to *Desperate Housewives*, have been shown driving Maseratis, too.

Tiki Barber inside a Quattroporte

New Maseratis

In 2009, Maserati showed off a new, four-seat convertible at the International Motor Show in Frankfurt, Germany. The car came out the next year. It was called the GranCabrio in Europe and the GranTurismo Convertible in North America.

The GranTurismo MC Stradale was introduced in 2011. It had a powerful 450-horsepower engine and was designed for a smooth drive. Like all the cars Maserati has made in the past few years, it brought the excitement of driving a Maserati to a whole new group of owners. The years to come are sure to bring more great Maseratis.

Today, Maserati sells three versions of its classic four-door car. They are the Quattroporte; the Quattroporte S, which has a slightly bigger engine; and the Quattroporte GT S, which is the most powerful.

The GranTurismo MC Stradale can go faster than 186 miles (299 km) per hour.

Glossary

aerodynamic: having a shape that improves airflow around a car to increase its speed

class: a group of cars with some of the same features

compress: to press or squeeze together

concept car: a car built to show a new design and features that may one day be used in cars sold to the public

convertible: a car with a roof that can be lowered or removed

coupe: a two-door car with one section for the seat and another for storage space

cylinder: the enclosed tube-shaped spaces in an engine where fuel is burned

design: to create the pattern or shape of something

gearshift: the part of the car that connects and disconnects the gears

horsepower: the measurement of an engine's power

hydraulic: having to do with a system powered by liquids moving through tubes

interior: inside

spyder: a two-seat car without a roof or side or rear windows. Also may be called a roadster.

straight-six: describing an engine with six cylinders arranged in a line. Also called an in-line six.

V-8: an engine with eight cylinders arranged in a V shape

For More Information

Books

Graham, Ian. *Fast Cars*. Mankato, MN: Smart Apple Media, 2009.

Maurer, Tracy. *Maserati*. Vero Beach, FL: Rouke Publishing, 2008.

Schaefer, A. R. *Maserati*. Mankato, MN: Capstone Press, 2008.

Websites

The History of the Maserati
www.maserati.us/maserati/us/en/index/passion/Heritage.html
Learn more about early Maseratis.

Maserati: Main Model List
www.italiancar.com.au/site/cars/maserati/models/MasModels.html
See pictures of many different Maseratis.

Publisher's note to educators and parents: Our editors have carefully reviewed these websites to ensure that they are suitable for students. Many websites change frequently, however, and we cannot guarantee that a site's future contents will continue to meet our high standards of quality and educational value. Be advised that students should be closely supervised whenever they access the Internet.

Index